EMMA REIN
ROBOT ENGINEER

WORDS BY
JENNY LU

PICTURES BY
GEORGE SWEETLAND

Hardcover ISBN: 978-1-7370647-0-1
Paperback ISBN: 978-1-7370647-1-8

For my husband, Edward, with love.

For my children, Ethan and Brandon, pursue your passion and follow your dreams.

Lulu Books

EMMA REN
ROBOT ENGINEER

WORDS BY
JENNY LU

PICTURES BY
GEORGE SWEETLAND

Emma grinned as Mrs. Lee wrote the weekly assignment on the board. She and her dad built things together all the time. This would be so easy and fun!

LARGE WHEELS

GRAPPLE CLAW

STRONG FRONT

Emma listened as Mrs. Lee described the steps they would take to build their robot.

"We will be working in pairs," Mrs. Lee continued. "At the end of the week, your robots will battle."

Emma looked around the room. She spotted Sophia and waved. They would make a great team!

But Mrs. Lee had other ideas. "Let's see. Sophia and Jake. Emma and Jeremy. Anna and—"

STEM ENGINEERING PROCESS
1 ASK 2 IMAGINE 3 PLAN
4 CREATE 5 TEST 6 IMPROVE

Emma's heart sank. Jeremy! "Oh, great. A girl," Emma heard him whisper. "What do girls know about robots?"

Emma felt her face turn red. How DARE Jeremy say something like that! The fact that she was a girl did not mean she could not build things! *I'll show him!*

As Emma scooted her chair over, she said, "So, what do we need our robot to do?" Jeremy rolled his eyes. "Beat the other robots. Obviously!"

Emma shook her head, "Our robot should have huge tires. That way, it can roll over obstacles."

Jeremy scowled at Emma.

"I'll decide what it's going to look like. You just draw it," he said.

As Jeremy gave her ideas, Emma drew out their robot.

"Let's add a lifter!" she suggested. "Our robot could use it to flip opponents over."

"We need something stronger than that," said Jeremy.

Emma drew a claw and showed it to Jeremy. "How about this?"

"Draw a cage around the robot," Jeremy said and ignored her suggestion.

"I don't think that's a good idea," Emma said. "A cage may be too heavy. It could slow the robot down."

"I told you, I'm deciding what the robot looks like. Robot building is for boys. Drawing is for girls."

He shoved the paper back toward her.

"Add a cage."

Finally, Jeremy and Emma agreed on a design for their robot.

Then, they had to create it.

Emma grabbed the huge wheels.

Jeremy gathered the frame, connectors, and motor.

Working together, they built their robot.

"I think it's missing something to help with defense," Emma said when they were done. "Let's add the claw. It can grab the other robot and lift it up."

Jeremy eyed Emma. "Fine," he said at last. "We'll add a claw. But if it messes with our robot, I'm telling Mrs. Lee it was your idea!"

Emma nodded. "Deal!"

Later, as Emma looked at the finished creation, she knew they had built the perfect robot.

On Friday, Emma's class came in to find a battle ring in the middle of the classroom. "You've all done a great job on your robots!" Mrs. Lee said. "Now, who's ready to battle?"

Emma put their robot, Claw Force, in the ring. It was up against Sophia's robot, Raptor 5.

Emma watched nervously, and her heart pounded to the beat of the stomping crowd. If Claw Force was trapped, the battle would be over!

Emma felt her shoulders tighten. She clenched her fists.

If only Jeremy had listened to her about adding a lifter, Claw Force could have flipped Raptor 5 over and won.

Suddenly, Jeremy called a time-out.

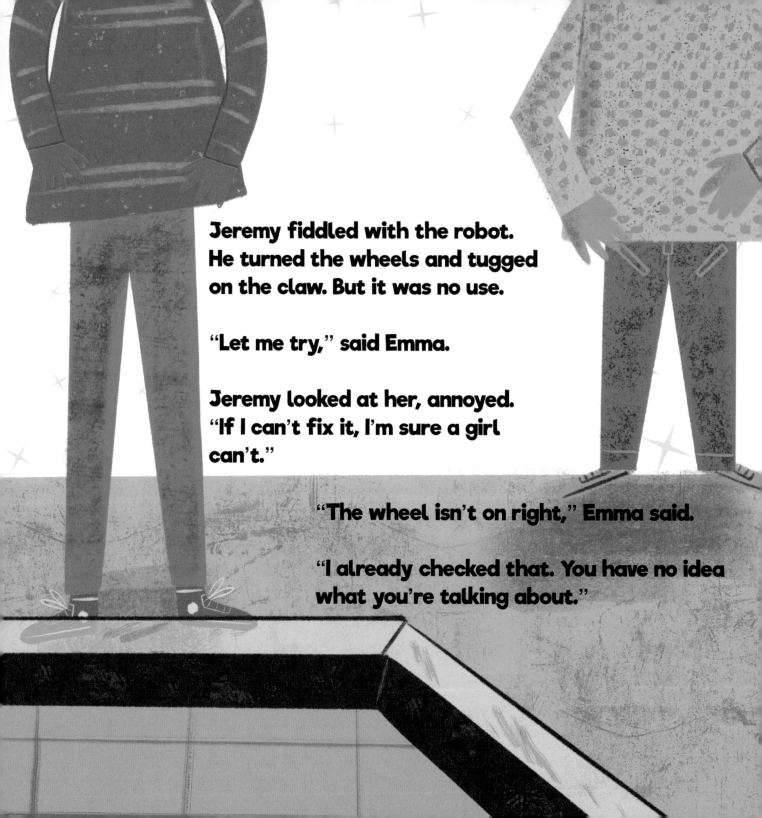

Jeremy fiddled with the robot. He turned the wheels and tugged on the claw. But it was no use.

"Let me try," said Emma.

Jeremy looked at her, annoyed. "If I can't fix it, I'm sure a girl can't."

"The wheel isn't on right," Emma said.

"I already checked that. You have no idea what you're talking about."

Emma crossed her arms.

"Listen, it's not working. If we put it back in, it's going to lose. So let me try. What's the worst that can happen?"

Jeremy grudgingly handed over the robot.

Emma loosened the wheel studs,

rotated the wheel,

and snapped it back on tight just as the timer went off.

BEEP! BEEP! BEEP! BEEP! BEEP! BEEP!

0:00

The time-out was over.

BEEP! BEEP! BEEP! BEEP! BEEP!

Emma held her breath and waited to see if Claw Force would move.

Claw Force slowly inched forward.

Raptor 5 sped toward it, then pushed Claw Force against the wall of the ring.
BANG! BASH! BAM!

Emma closed her eyes.
It was over!

Just then, the crowd whooped and cheered.
Emma opened her eyes. Claw Force had spun around and
moved faster!

It pushed Raptor 5 hard, smashing it against the other
side of the ring.

BOOM
BANG
BOOM BOOM
BANG
BOOM

Raptor 5 lost its spinner and a wheel. Then, Claw Force grabbed the other robot with its claw and lifted it up in the air. It dropped Raptor 5 to the floor and broke it into a thousand pieces.

Emma could not believe it. Claw Force won!

All around her, Emma's classmates cheered, "Emma, Emma, Emma!"

Emma turned to give Jeremy a high-five. To her surprise, he smiled at her.

"You were right about the wheel," he said. "I'm sorry I didn't listen. You're great at building and fixing things."

Emma held her head high. "Thanks," she said with a smile. "You're not so bad yourself."

"Hey, how about we build another robot? We can use what we learned from Claw Force to build an even better one!" Jeremy said. "And this time, I promise to listen to your suggestions."

Emma grinned. She was glad Jeremy realized that building robots was not just for boys.

"I can't wait!"

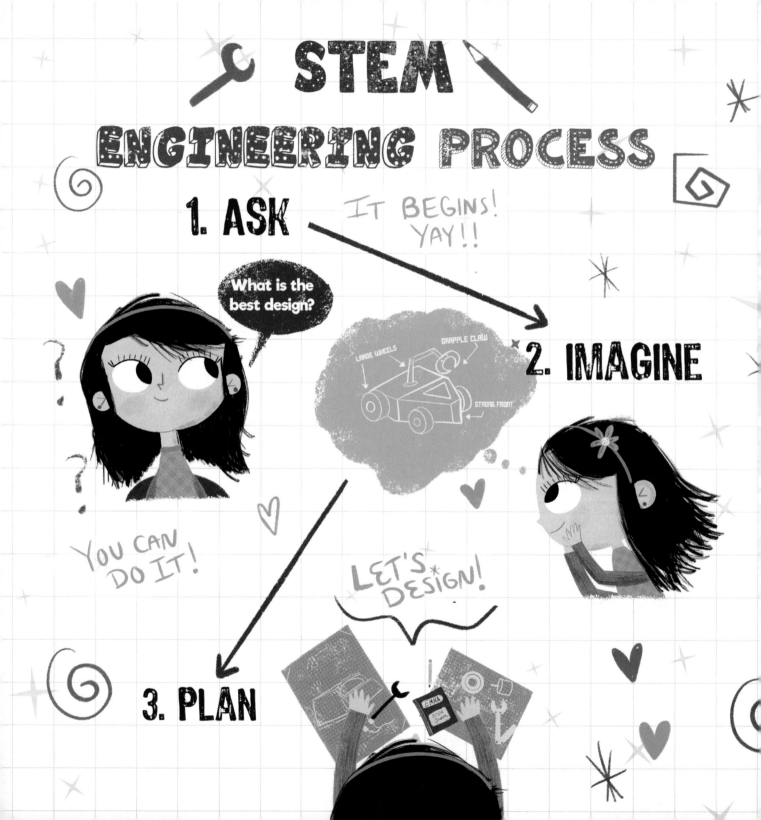

Made in the USA
Las Vegas, NV
09 November 2021

34063321R00026